DISNEY'S THE VILLAINS COLLECTION

by Todd Strasser

with poems by Mark Rifkin

illustrated by Gil DiCicco

Disney PRESS

New York

To my good friend Rebecca Gilbert, who is in no way a villain
—T.S.

For Grandpa Moe and Grandma Ida, with love
—M.D.R.

"I've Got No Strings"
from Walt Disney's *Pinocchio*
Lyric by Ned Washington Music by Leigh Harline
Copyright © 1940 by Bourne Co.
Copyright Renewed
International Copyright Secured All rights Reserved
Used by Permission

"The Elegant Captain Hook"
from Walt Disney's *Peter Pan*
Words by Sammy Cahn
Music by Sammy Fain
Copyright ©1952 Walt Disney Music Company
Copyright Renewed
Used by Permission All Rights Reserved

First Edition
1 3 5 7 9 10 8 6 4 2

Library of Congress Catalog Card Number: 93-70882
ISBN 1-56282-500-3/1-56282-501-1 (lib. bdg.)

Disney's

THE **VILLAINS** COLLECTION

TABLE OF CONTENTS

THE VILLAINS COLLECTION

Disney's

THE

COLLECTION

MIRROR, MIRROR

Mirror, mirror, on the wall,
how can I *not* be the fairest of all?
Do not speak again of that awful Snow White ~
she's nothing more than a hideous sight!

Her smile is not nearly as pretty as mine,
and her black hair does have the most ludicrous shine.
I've dressed her in rags, for in rags she should be ~
don't tell me that sad girl is fairer than me!

Snow White is naught but a scullery maid ~
my wish to be rid of her shan't be delayed!
She's a pitiable child, a miserable shrew ~
I can't wait to bid her a final adieu!

I command you, O mirror, watch out what you say!
If you speak of Snow White it is time you should pray!
For if ever again should you dare breathe that name ~
I'll tear you to pieces and smash up your frame!

WHO'S THE FAIREST ONE OF ALL?

ONE DAY, WHEN THE EVIL QUEEN ASKED her magic mirror the usual question—"Who is the fairest one of all?"—she got an unexpected reply. "Snow White," said the face in the mirror. Enraged that her stepdaughter was more beautiful than she, the jealous queen ordered her huntsman to kill the young princess and bring back her heart as proof.

*   *   *

Now the queen stood, once again, before the oval mirror in its gold frame. In her hands she held a small red box. It was clasped with a golden sword that pierced a golden heart. The huntsman had assured her that Snow White's heart lay inside.

"Magic mirror on the wall," the queen said. "Who *now* is the fairest one of all?"

As before, a hazy face appeared in the mirror, and this time the voice replied, "Over the seven jeweled hills, beyond the seventh fall, in the cottage of the seven dwarfs, dwells Snow White, fairest one of all."

Surely the mirror was mistaken, the queen thought.

"But Snow White lies dead in the forest," she said, opening the box. "The huntsman has brought me proof. Behold, her heart."

"Snow White still lives, the fairest in the land," the face in the mirror replied. "'Tis the heart of a pig you hold in your hand."

"The heart of a pig?" The queen's face reddened with

anger as she stared into the box. "I've been tricked!"

In a rage she turned away from the mirror and descended the stone steps toward the cellar of the castle. There she pulled open a heavy wooden door and entered her laboratory. The shadowy room was lit by flickering candles. Tables were covered with bubbling beakers and flasks. The walls were lined with dusty shelves filled with books of ancient magic spells and formulas.

"The heart of a pig!" the queen cried in disgust, flinging the box away. "The huntsman was a blundering fool. I'll go myself to the dwarfs' cottage in a disguise so complete that Snow White will never suspect who I am."

The queen reached into a bookcase for an old leather-bound book. "Now for a formula to transform my beauty into ugliness," she said, turning the worn pages. "I'll change my queenly gown to a peddler's cloak."

Adding ingredients to a mixing glass as she read, the queen concocted a potion.

"Mummy dust to make me old," she chanted. "To shroud my clothes, the black of night. To age my voice, an old hag's cackle. To whiten my hair—a scream of fright!"

The ingredients blended into a black liquid inside the beaker. With a terrible shriek, a ghostly vapor rose from the glass. The queen held the beaker high and stepped to the open window.

"A blast of wind to fan my hate," she cried. "A thunder-bolt to mix it with. Now begin thy magic spell!" Wind roared through the window, blowing out the candles and sending the room into darkness. Lightning flashed as the queen drank the potion and hurled the empty beaker to the floor with a crash.

Her throat burned, and her stomach was knotted in pain. Her hands grew into long gnarled claws, and her hair turned wiry and white. Her voice became a hoarse rasp, and her nose grew long and warted. Her eyes bulged horribly, and all but one tooth fell out of her deformed jaw.

Now a hideous witch, she cackled with delight. The time had come to devise an especially cruel fate for Snow White. Thumbing through the pages of the book, she found the perfect spell—a poisoned apple that, when eaten, would cause the sleeping death.

Soon she was stirring a cauldron filled with a glowing, bubbling liquid. In her other hand she held a single green apple.

"Dip the apple in the brew," she intoned, lowering the apple into the froth. "Let the sleeping death seep through."

As the poison dripped off the apple, a skull appeared on its skin.

"Look!" the witch cried. "On the skin, a symbol of what lies within. Now turn red to tempt Snow White, make her hunger for a bite. When she breaks the tender peel to taste the apple in my hand, her breath will still, her blood will congeal. Then I'll be the fairest in the land!" The apple turned a glowing red.

"But wait! What if there's an antidote?" she said in a low voice. The witch flipped through the pages of her book once again.

"Ah! I was right," she cried, her bony finger following the lines on the dingy page. "The victim of the sleeping death can be revived only by love's first kiss.

"Bah!" she grumbled. "No fear of that. The dwarfs will think she's dead—she'll be buried alive! Buried alive! Buried alive!" the witch cackled over and over again.

Finally, she placed the poisoned apple in a basket of ordinary apples and hurried toward the forest.

"The little men will be off at work, and Snow White will be alone with a harmless old peddler woman," she whispered to herself. Through the trees ahead she could see the dwarfs' stone cottage. Her mouth split into a menacing grin.

A moment later the witch leaned in the open window. Inside, Snow White was busy making a pie crust.

"All alone, my pet?" the witch asked with a chuckle.

"Oh! Why yes, I am," the pretty girl replied uneasily.

"The little men aren't here?" the witch asked just to be certain.

"No, they're not."

"Hmmm." The witch sniffed the air with her long crooked nose. "Making pies?"

"Yes," Snow White said as she continued to work. "Gooseberry pies."

"It's apple pies that makes menfolk's mouths water," the witch said, taking the poisoned apple from her basket. "Pies made from apples like this."

Snow White paused to look at the shiny red apple. "Oh, it does look delicious."

"Like to taste it?" the witch asked, offering the apple to the girl. "Go on, dearie, have a bite."

Snow White was just about to take the apple when a flock of friendly bluebirds swooped down from the trees and knocked the apple from the witch's hand. Circling wildly, they pecked at her head and neck until finally the witch lost her balance and fell to the ground.

"Oh no! Go away!" the witch cried, and waved her hands at the birds as she searched the ground for the apple. Not suspecting the danger, Snow White rushed out of the cottage and shooed the birds away.

"Stop it! Go away!" she scolded the birds. "Shame on you for frightening a poor old lady."

The witch found the apple and carefully dusted it off. Snow White helped her to her feet and apologized for the birds' odd behavior. But the witch knew why the birds had attacked her. The only way to escape them would be to go inside the cottage.

"Oh, my heart! My poor heart!" she cried. "Please take me into the house. Let me rest. A drink of water, please."

Just as the witch had hoped, Snow White led her inside, closing the door behind them to keep the birds out. After

Snow White gave her some water to drink, the witch pretended to regain her strength.

"Since you've been so good to poor old granny," she said, rising and holding out the apple, "I'll share a secret with you. This is no ordinary apple. It's a magic wishing apple. One bite and all your dreams will come true."

"Really?" Snow White's eyes widened.

"Yes, girlie," the witch replied. "Now make a wish and take a bite. There must be something your little heart desires."

But instead of taking a bite, Snow White backed away apprehensively. The witch stepped forward, still offering the apple. "Perhaps there's someone you love?"

Snow White hesitated. "Well, there is someone."

"I thought so!" the witch grinned. "Old granny knows a young girl's heart. Now take the apple and make a wish."

To the witch's wicked delight, Snow White cautiously accepted the apple. "I wish . . . ," she began, but paused.

"That's it!" the witch urged her. "Go on, go on!"

"I wish that he'd carry me away to his castle, where we will live happily ever after," Snow White said.

"Fine, fine," the witch said impatiently. "Now take a bite."

But Snow White still hesitated. The witch couldn't wait another second.

"Go on," she pressed the girl. "Don't let the wish grow cold."

She held her breath and watched as Snow White took a bite of the apple. Finally! A moment later the girl put her hand on her forehead.

"Oh, I feel so strange." Snow White's voice was barely a whisper.

The witch rubbed her gnarled hands with evil delight as Snow White lost her balance and staggered. "Her breath will still, her blood will congeal. . . ."

The apple fell out of Snow White's hand. A moment later she tumbled to the floor. The witch stood over her, cackling victoriously. "Now I'll be the fairest in the land!"

ONLY THE FINEST!

Iago, my friend, the throne shall be ours~
we will rule over all of the land!
Diamonds and rubies and sapphires galore~
we'll have it all, just like we planned!

The sultan's no more than a blithering fool~
a jester whose power is lame!
His daughter's a vain and impetuous girl~
but I'll marry her just the same!

Then when we get our hands on the lamp
nothing will stand in our way!
The entire kingdom will suffer our wrath~
we'll make every last one of them pay!

Another stale cracker, you'll never choke down~
for us there'll be only the finest!
No more will we bow to the sultan, that clown~
for soon *all* will call *me* Your Highness!

MASTER OF THE LAMP

❖

CLUTCHING THE MAGIC LAMP in his long, bony fingers, Jafar stared down at the crowded palace courtyard with a wickedly triumphant smile on his face. Below, Aladdin, disguised as Prince Ali Ababwa, stood with Princess Jasmine and the sultan on the gold-canopied balcony of the the royal palace. Little did the street rat know that he no longer possessed the lamp and the powers of the genie.

Jafar snickered at the thought of what he was about to do. "So, Iago," he said to his parrot, "Princess Jasmine has finally chosen her precious prince."

"Yeah, look at them cheering that little pip-squeak!" Iago cried.

"Let them cheer," Jafar replied as he rubbed the lamp. "From now on the power of the genie is mine!"

With a flash the great blue genie appeared. When he saw who had rubbed the lamp, he looked puzzled.

"*I* am your master now!" Jafar barked.

"I was afraid of that," the genie replied.

"Keep quiet!" the evil adviser shouted. "And now, slave, grant me my first wish. I wish to rule as sultan!"

The genie had no choice but to comply. Reddish black clouds instantly swirled over the castle. Gusting winds ripped the canopy off the balcony. Suddenly the kindly old sultan

was engulfed in a strange, swirling mist.

"What is it?" the sultan gasped. "What's going on?"

"Father!" Jasmine cried as her father disappeared from sight.

A moment later Jafar stood on the balcony wearing the sultan's robes. Even Iago now wore a sultan's turban. The sultan himself was cast aside in only his underwear. A loud gasp rose from the crowd.

"Jafar!" the sultan shouted. "You vile betrayer!"

"You will address him as *Sultan* Jafar," Iago sneered.

"Oh yeah? We'll see about that," Aladdin said, stepping toward the impostor. But seeing the magic lamp in Jafar's hands, he suddenly stopped. "The lamp!"

"That's right," Jafar said with a sly grin. "I have the ultimate power now."

A huge shadow fell across the courtyard as the genie reached down. Wrapping his hands around the palace, he lifted it off the ground and flew toward a mountain, high above the city. The crowd screamed and scattered as debris tumbled down around them.

"Genie . . . No!" Aladdin shouted.

"Sorry, kid," the genie replied sadly. "I've got a new master now."

"Jafar, I order you to stop!" the sultan shouted angrily.

"There's a new order now," Jafar replied. "My order! Finally, you will bow to me!"

"We will *never* bow to you!" Princess Jasmine shouted.

Taken aback, Jafar scowled angrily at them. "If you won't bow, then you will cower! Genie, for my second wish you will make me the most powerful sorcerer in the world!"

Jafar felt a strange, electrifying force surge through him. In his hand his snake-headed staff grew larger and crackled with green light. Jasmine's pet tiger, Rajah, roared and leapt at the sorcerer-sultan. But Jafar simply waved his staff, and Rajah was instantly transformed into a small kitten, his once-mighty roar now a mere meow.

"Leave them alone, Jafar!" Aladdin shouted.

Jafar glared at Aladdin with evil glee. "Oh, Princess," he said smugly. "There's someone I'm dying to introduce you to. Say hello to your precious Prince Ali."

"Or should we say, Aladdin," Iago taunted.

A bolt of green light flashed from the staff. Prince Ali's elephant instantly became Abu the monkey once again. Aladdin's princely clothes vanished, leaving him in the rags he'd worn in the streets.

"See? He's nothing more than a worthless lying street rat," Jafar sneered.

"Why did you lie to me?" Jasmine looked at Aladdin, now the boy she recognized from the marketplace.

But before Aladdin could explain, Jafar used his sorcery to lift the boy and his monkey off the ground and into a nearby tower window. Then, with a swing of his staff, he sent the tower rocketing high into the air. "So long, Prince Ali Abooboo!" Jafar cried.

"At last," Jafar laughed and shouted, "Agrabah is mine!"

*　*　*

Surrounded by vast piles of gold and jewels in his new throne room, Jafar glanced contentedly out his window at the cloudy mountaintops that now surrounded his palace. As the genie massaged his feet, Jafar sipped wine from a golden goblet and turned his gaze to the former sultan, now dressed in a jester's costume and suspended from the ceiling like a marionette.

Near Jafar, Princess Jasmine sat with her wrists shackled. Jafar hooked the chains with his staff and pulled her close.

"It pains me to see you reduced to this, Jasmine," he said with a leer. "A beautiful desert bloom such as yourself should be on the arm of the most powerful sultan in the world." With a wave of his staff, he transformed her chains into a golden crown. "What do you say, my dear?"

Jasmine grabbed the goblet from his hand and splashed the wine in his face. *"Never!"* she cried.

Enraged, Jafar jumped up from his cobra-shaped throne. "I'll teach you some respect!" he shouted, and turned to the genie. "For my final wish, you will make Princess Jasmine fall in love with me!"

"But I can't make anyone fall in love, Master," the genie stammered.

"Don't talk back to me, you big blue lout!" Jafar shouted, grabbing the genie by his thin black beard. "You will do what I order you to do, slave."

"Jafar," Jasmine said, her voice suddenly silky. "I never realized how handsome you are."

"That's better," Jafar said with a smile, and moved closer to the princess. "Now, pussycat, tell me more about myself."

"You're tall and dark," Jasmine said, sliding her arms around him. "You've stolen my heart."

"And the street rat?" Jafar asked, referring to Aladdin.

"What street rat?" Jasmine purred.

In the background Jafar thought he heard a crash, but before he could turn to see what it was, Jasmine pulled him close and kissed him. Finally, the evil sultan pulled back, dazed with joy. But as his eyes focused, he saw the reflection of Aladdin in Jasmine's shiny new crown.

What the devil! The embrace, the kiss . . . it had all been a trick! "You!" Jafar turned and blasted Aladdin with his staff, sending him hurtling into a pile of jewels. "How many times do I have to kill you, boy?"

Jafar aimed the staff again. The first blast was meant to stun, the second was meant to destroy. Suddenly Jasmine lunged at him, knocking the staff aside. Jafar spun around. "You deceiving shrew!" he snarled. "Your time is up!"

With a blast of light, Jasmine was trapped in the bottom of a giant hourglass. Sand pouring down from the top threatened to bury her alive. Jafar aimed his staff at Abu next. *Zap!* The monkey instantly became a cymbal-clanking toy.

Now the sorcerer turned his staff, once again, on Aladdin. In a flash, dozens of razor-sharp swords materialized above Aladdin's head and began to rain down on him. Aladdin managed to dodge each one, but suddenly a wall of fire burst from the floor. Jafar stepped toward the boy, forcing him back toward the roaring flames.

"Afraid to fight me yourself, you cowardly snake?" Aladdin taunted him, grabbing one of the swords and brandishing it at Jafar.

"A snake, am I?" Jafar replied with a haughty laugh. "Perhaps you'd like to see how snakelike I can be!"

Jafar gripped his staff with both hands and appeared to flow into it. At the same time, the staff grew into a giant cobra with black skin and red eyes and terrifyingly long fangs. Aladdin tried to battle him, but it was no use. Soon he was trapped within the serpent's mighty coils.

Meanwhile, in the giant hourglass, Princess Jasmine was all but buried under the sand.

"You little fool," Jafar hissed as he slowly crushed the air

out of Aladdin's lungs. "You thought you could outwit the most powerful being on earth?"

Caught in the slowly tightening coils, Aladdin gasped for a breath he couldn't take. "Squeeze him, Jafar," Iago whispered with cruel delight. "Squeeze him!"

A Very Fine Fur

There is nothing like stroking a fur,
with its softness surrounding your throat.
Rabbit and sable I already have~
what I want is a Dalmatian coat!

Ninety-nine Dalmatian puppies, I think,
will fit me to a T.
One by one, I'll gather them up
and wrap them all around me!

Then in my fabulous brand-new fur coat,
I'll flaunt myself all over town.
If I like it enough, well then, who knows?
Perhaps next a Dalmatian gown!

PUPPY CAPER

CRUELLA DE VIL SAT IN HER PINK BED with her stringy white-and-black hair in rollers. Puffing on a cigarette, she picked up the morning paper. DOGNAPPING read the headline in bold black letters. Under the headline was a photograph of Cruella's old schoolmate, Anita, with her husband, Roger, and their nanny, gazing sadly at an empty puppy basket.

"Dognapping! Can you imagine?" Cruella cried. "Why, who could have stolen those fifteen darling little puppies?" she laughed, knowing full well that Horace and Jasper Badun had done the crafty deed. After all, she had masterminded the job herself. If Roger refused to sell her the puppies, what other choice did she have? She simply *had* to steal them. No one was going to stop Cruella De Vil from having a Dalmatian fur coat!

She looked at the newspaper photograph again. "Anita and her bashful Beethoven, pipe and all!" Cruella laughed harshly. "Oh, Roger, you are a fool."

Her laughter was interrupted by the ringing of the phone beside her bed. Cruella answered. It was Jasper. Cruella became irate.

"Jasper, you idiot!" she snarled. "How dare you call me here!"

But Jasper wanted the money she'd promised him for stealing the pups.

"Not one shilling until the job is done!" Cruella shouted. "Do you understand?"

Horace and Jasper were nervous. They had also seen the newspapers. "Hang the papers," Cruella screeched into the phone, "It'll be forgotten by tomorrow, you imbeciles!" Cruella slammed the receiver down but quickly picked it up again and dialed Anita's number.

Roger answered, mumbling something about an inspector, but Cruella asked for Anita.

"Hello?" Anita said.

"Anita, darling, what a terrible thing," Cruella said, trying her best to sound sympathetic. "I just saw it in the papers. I simply couldn't believe it."

"Yes, Cruella," Anita sounded subdued. "It was quite a shock."

"Have you called the police?" Cruella asked.

"Yes, we've called Scotland Yard," Anita replied.

Suddenly Roger grabbed the phone away from his wife and shouted, "Where are they?"

Before Cruella could reply that she had no idea what he was talking about, Anita took the phone back and apologized.

"Well," Cruella said with a huff, as if she was insulted by Roger's accusations. "If there's any news, you'll let me know, won't you?"

Anita said she would and hung up. On the other end

Cruella slammed the phone down. *Scotland Yard!* Blast it, she never expected Roger and Anita to go that far. And the way Roger had grabbed the phone away and accused her of taking the pups. . . . It sounded as if he was suspicious.

Suddenly Cruella knew what she had to do. She jumped out of bed, threw on her clothes, and hurried to her car. It had started to snow, but she was driving to the mansion tonight!

*   *   *

Hours later Cruella arrived at her large gloomy estate. She quickly let herself in and found Horace and Jasper sitting on an old sofa watching television. They were surrounded by dozens of Dalmatian puppies.

"It's got to be done tonight," Cruella shouted at the Baduns.

They were so busy watching a game show that Cruella couldn't tell if they'd heard her or not. She stepped to the television and blocked their view.

"Do you understand?" she shouted. "Tonight!"

"Huh? But they ain't big enough," Horace argued, trying to glance around her at the TV.

"You couldn't get more than half a dozen coats from the whole caboodle," Jasper added as he took a swig from a bottle.

"Then I'll settle for half a dozen!" Cruella shouted, waving her arms. "We can't wait. The police are everywhere! I want the job done tonight!"

"How are we going to do it?" Horace asked.

"Any way you like!" Cruella shouted. "Poison them, drown them, bash their heads in! I don't care how you kill the little beasts. Just do it! And do it now!"

To her absolute amazement, Jasper glanced back at the television. "Please, miss," he begged. "Have some pity. Can't we see the rest of the show first?"

"Yeah," Horace added. "We want to see 'What's My Crime?'"

Jasper started to take another drink from the bottle. Infuriated, Cruella grabbed it out of his hands and emptied it over his face. Then she threw the bottle into the fireplace, where it shattered against the bricks.

"Now listen, you idiots!" she screamed, slapping them both. "I'll be back first thing in the morning. And the job had better be done, or *I'll* call the police. Understand?"

The Baduns responded with frightened nods. Cruella spun around and stormed out of the room, slamming the door so hard that a piece of plaster broke loose from the ceiling and crashed down on Horace's head.

Sweet Revenge!

Ahoy, my mateys, and tallyho!
It's time to set sail—look high and look low!
Come Mullins and Smee and every last man!
We'll search round the world till I find Peter Pan!

That boy hasn't seen the last of me yet!
I'll get him and his friends—on that you can bet!
Then I'll cut him to ribbons, that poor little fool~
He thinks he can beat mighty Hook in a duel!

He'll walk down that plank, the miserable clown!
How proud I will stand as I watch Peter drown!
Yes, watching him die will be such a treat!
Oh, revenge can taste so wonderfully sweet!

PIRATES, OR THE PLANK!

ON BOARD THE PIRATE SHIP, Hook ordered his men to tie Wendy and the boys to the mast with heavy ropes. It would be quite easy to get rid of them, but the pirate captain had other plans. He needed more pirates for his crew, and certainly the boys were young and impressionable. He would figure out what to do with the girl later.

On the deck before them, the pirates danced and sang of the fun it was to be a pirate:

So try the life of a thief,
Just sample the life of a crook.
There isn't a boy who won't enjoy
A-workin' with Captain Hook!

The captain looked down at the hook that took the place of his left hand. Finally, he would have his revenge against Peter Pan for feeding his hand to the crocodile years ago. It wouldn't be long before that nuisance, Pan, would be out of the way for good.

Wearing his best red coat and a pirate hat with a long white plume, Hook made a special offer to his guests.

"Sign on as a pirate today and you'll get a free tattoo," he

announced with a sly smile. The boys laughed as a muscular pirate flexed his biceps, making a tattoo of a black skull and crossbones flutter.

Once again Hook got their attention. "Now boys," he warned, "I'll be frank. If you don't sign up, you'll walk the plank!"

Hook pointed at the long wooden gangplank. Just as he had hoped, the boys' eyes went wide with fear. Once again the pirates began to dance and sing:

The choice is up to you.
You'll love the life of a thief.
You'll relish the life of a crook.
There's barrels of fun for everyone.
And you'll get treasures by the ton.
So come on and sign the book.
Join up with Captain Hook.

Across the deck, Hook sat down at a desk with his pirate book and dipped a feather quill in a pot of ink. "Free the boys," he ordered.

A pirate near the mast cut the rope. Hook was delighted as the boys started to race across the deck toward him, eager to join the crew.

"Boys!" Wendy yelled, clapping her hands sharply. "Aren't you ashamed of yourselves?"

To Hook's astonishment, the boys skidded to a halt and turned back to her.

"But Captain Hook is most insistent," John, the older of Wendy's brothers, tried to explain.

"Yeah," said Cubby, a Lost Boy who was dressed in bearskin. "If we don't sign up, he said we'll walk the plank!"

"Oh no we won't." Wendy waved a finger at them and defiantly turned her nose up at the pirate captain. "Peter Pan will save us."

Hook turned to Smee and mimicked the girl. "She said Peter Pan will save them, Smee."

The captain and his mate laughed heartily and fell into each other's arms. Little did the girl know! Finally, Hook turned to Wendy, tipped his hat, and bowed.

"A thousand pardons, my dear," Hook said with feigned chivalry. "I don't believe you're in on our little joke. You see, we left a present for Peter Pan."

"A sort of surprise package, you might say," Smee added.

"And could Peter see within the package," Hook went on, "he would find an ingenious time bomb that will blast him out of Never Land forever!"

"Oh no! No!" Wendy gasped.

"Yes!" the pirate captain cried, holding a clock up by his silver hook and counting down the seconds.

Suddenly Never Land was shaken by an explosion so great that tree trunks and huge rocks were hurtled hundreds of yards in the air. Out in the cove the pirate ship rocked sideways. Wendy and the boys watched aghast as black smoke filled the sky.

Hook could hardly contain his delight. Finally, he'd gotten rid of that nuisance, Peter Pan! As Wendy and the boys looked back at the island in stunned silence, the pirate captain took off his hat and held it over his heart.

"And so passeth a worthy opponent," he said with mock solemnity, pretending to wipe a tear from his eye. But a split second later he reached for the feather quill.

"So which will it be?" he asked. "The pen . . . or the plank?"

"We will never join your crew," Wendy stated bravely.

Fine, thought Hook. Perhaps it was best to get rid of them.

"As you wish," he replied with a malicious grin, and pointed at the plank. "Ladies first, my dear."

The end was near, but Wendy remained brave and calm. She turned to the Lost Boys and said good-bye, then turned to her brothers. "Be brave, John."

"I shall strive to, Wendy." John stood tall and puffed out his chest, but he was very sad.

Michael wiped a tear from his eye, and Wendy gave him a farewell kiss on the cheek.

The pirate captain had had enough of this tender scene. He gave a sign to one of his men, who immediately grabbed the girl and shoved her across the deck. "Go on with ya!"

Hook ordered the boys tied to the mast again so that they wouldn't interfere as his men pushed Wendy toward the plank. The pirate captain watched with cruel anticipation as the girl held her head high and walked slowly out over the dark, foaming waters. Behind her the bloodthirsty pirates shouted impatiently.

Hook smiled. There was nothing quite so lovely as seeing someone go off the plank. His heart leapt with joy as Wendy took her last step and promptly disappeared.

FEAR MY WRATH!

How dare they not invite me
to Aurora's birthday bash!
Amid a burst of lightning
I'll show up in a flash!

To think that Merryweather,
in that awful dress of blue,
is on the royal guest list~
I should be on it, too!

Oh, those three annoying fairies
are not so very good.
Why am *I* not invited?
I'm so misunderstood!

They think they can forget me?
I've warned them all before!
Well, this time I am coming~
they'll leave me out no more!

The time is growing closer,
my revenge is drawing near~
soon all within the kingdom
will be screaming out in fear!

A BIRTHDAY SURPRISE

WITHIN THE DAMP, DARK CRUMBLING STONE WALLS of her castle, high atop a craggy peak, Maleficent waited anxiously as the sun began to set. For sixteen years she'd had her goons search for Princess Aurora without any luck. Now there was little time left to capture the princess, let alone to bring her evil spell to pass. Maleficent thought back to the day of the little princess's birth. How dare the king and queen not invite her to the celebration. They had even invited those three annoyingly good fairies, Flora, Fauna, and Merryweather! She recalled the curse she'd placed on the baby that very day: Aurora would prick her finger on the spindle of a spinning wheel and die before her sixteenth birthday. Now if she could only find the girl!

Maleficent knew her raven was her last hope. She'd sent her pet into the sky to search for a fair maid of sixteen, with hair of sunshine gold and lips as red as a rose. Maleficent tapped her gold-tipped staff impatiently against the stone floor. Time was running out.

Suddenly she heard a distant flapping of wings. A moment later the black bird glided through the decaying castle and landed on its master's hand.

"Have you found her?" Maleficent demanded. The bird

nodded and whispered in the evil witch's ear.

"She's been living with those three fairies in the woods all these years? They've named her Briar Rose?" Maleficent's dark eyes widened in amazement. "You say that tonight they're taking the princess back to King Stefan's castle so that she can marry the prince?"

Again the bird nodded its shiny black head. A wicked smile curled onto Maleficent's bright red lips. "We'll see about that."

*   *   *

In a room inside the castle the princess sat before a dressing table, her new crown on her head. The three good fairies sat on a bench outside the room, giving Princess Aurora a moment alone before taking her back to her real parents, the king and queen. But she was not alone.

A fire crackled in the hearth not far from where Princess Aurora sat. With a silent burst, the flames grew bright and then went out, leaving a glowing, snakelike wisp of green smoke rising from the ashes. From within the wisp of smoke, Maleficent's power silently beckoned to the princess.

Instantly under the witch's spell, Aurora rose from the table in a trance and walked slowly toward the hearth. Her eyes were wide and glassy as she approached the glowing orb in the fireplace. Luring Aurora on, Maleficent created an opening behind the fireplace for the princess to step through.

The evil witch continued to lead the entranced princess up a dark winding stairway in one of the castle's turrets. Maleficent knew there was no time to lose. Those three meddling fairies had already discovered that the princess was

gone. Now their searching voices echoed through the halls below as they cried, "Briar Rose! Briar Rose!"

Finally, the evil witch led the princess into a room at the top of the turret. There Maleficent quickly created a wooden spinning wheel with an eerie green spindle. Princess Aurora stepped forward, slowly raising a hand and an outstretched finger.

The voices of the good fairies echoed up the stone stairwell and into the room. "Don't touch anything!"

Faintly hearing their calls, Princess Aurora pulled her hand back. But Maleficent's dark magic was stronger.

"Touch the spindle!" she ordered. "Touch it now, I say!"

The princess again reached her arm forward. Her finger touched the sharp point of the spindle.

Suddenly the entire room began to radiate with an eerie green light. A moment later Flora, Fauna, and Merryweather burst in. But it was too late. Maleficent stood before them with her flowing cape outstretched, her eyes shining with cruel satisfaction.

"You poor simple fools," she glowered at the fairies. "Thinking you could defeat me. . . . Me, the Mistress of All Evil! Well, here's your precious princess!"

The witch pulled in her cape, and the good fairies gasped in horror at what they saw. Maleficent cackled with wicked glee and disappeared in a blaze of green flames, leaving Princess Aurora lying motionless on the cold stone floor.

Gold Galore!

Come, my children,
gather round,
come hear him as he sings.
Pinocchio,
the wooden boy,
will dance without his strings!

Little does this
poor boy know
he now belongs to me.
He thinks he can
go home tonight,
but I'll never set him free!

A fortune he will
make for me
until he gets too old.
Then I'll chop him
into firewood
and count up all my gold!

NO STRINGS ATTACHED

❖

STROMBOLI COULDN'T BELIEVE HIS EYES! Before him stood a wooden puppet, ready to perform in his puppet show. But this was no ordinary puppet—this puppet was alive! He called himself Pinocchio, and he could walk, talk, sing, and dance without any strings. Stromboli rubbed his plump hands together. This little wooden boy could make him a fortune, certainly. Stromboli could already see the crowd gathering in the theater—and he could already visualize the stacks of gold coins. . . .

*   *   *

Later that night, while the rain poured down outside, Stromboli sat at the table in the back of his wagon, singing happily:

> *I got no strings but I got a brain.*
> *I buy a suit and I swing a cane.*
> *I eat the best and I drink champagne. . . .*

Pinocchio's first performance had been a big hit, indeed. As Stromboli sang, he speared several slices of meat and cheese with the point of a long, sharp knife and slid them into his mouth. Then he laughed to himself and looked across the table to where Pinocchio sat, watching him.

"Bravo, Pinocchio," cheered the large man loudly.

"They liked me," Pinocchio said with boyish excitement. The cheers and laughter of the crowd that night were still ringing in his ears.

"Hmmmmm." Stromboli nodded and looked down at the mound of gold coins in front of him.

With the tip of the knife, he slid a stack of coins to his left. "Two hundred," he mumbled to himself with pleasure. The crowd more than liked this silly wooden boy, he thought. *They loved him!* Stromboli knew that as long as Pinocchio worked for him, he would make a great deal of money.

"You are sensational!" the showman cried happily, and speared a green olive with his knife.

"You mean, I'm good?" Pinocchio asked innocently.

Stromboli smiled to himself and slid another stack of coins to his left. "Ah, three hundred." He turned to Pinocchio. "You are colossal!"

As he said this, he chopped a loaf of bread so hard that the piece he cut off bounced into the air. Stromboli speared the bread with his knife and then added an onion.

"Does that mean I'm an actor?" Pinocchio asked.

"Sure," Stromboli said. "I will push you into the public's eye." He picked the boy up and held him close as if he wanted to kiss him. "Your face, she will be on everybody's tongue!"

Stromboli dropped the boy back on the table. "Will she?" Pinocchio asked in awe.

"Yes—" Suddenly Stromboli's good cheer vanished. Lying in the middle of the large pile of gold was a fake gray coin. "What's this?" he growled angrily, placing the coin between his teeth and bending it.

Someone had slipped him a counterfeit coin! Stromboli was enraged. How dare they! The showman began to rant loudly, then remembered that he was sitting with the boy who would make him millions. His lips curled into a smile.

"For you, my little Pinocchio," he said, handing the bad coin to Pinocchio. Then he leaned back and drank from a bottle.

"For me?" Pinocchio gasped happily. "Gee, thanks! I'll go right home and tell Father."

"Home?" Stromboli nearly choked. Surely the boy was making a joke. "Oh, ho, ho, sure! Going home to your father!" Stromboli held his great belly and laughed. "That is very comical!"

Pinocchio was just about to jump off the table and head home. "You mean, it's funny?"

"Sure," Stromboli said.

Pinocchio laughed and tipped his hat to Stromboli as he said good-bye. "I'll be back in the morning."

Stromboli could hardly believe his ears. "Back in the morning!" he repeated, fighting the sudden desire to grab the boy. Instead he picked up Pinocchio gently and forced another laugh.

"Going home?" Still laughing and pretending he thought it was all very funny, Stromboli carried Pinocchio across the room. He stopped suddenly beside a wooden birdcage hanging from the ceiling. Without warning, he threw Pinocchio into the cage and locked it.

"There!" he shouted at the stunned boy. "This will be

your home . . . where I can always find you."

Pinocchio jumped to his feet and grasped the bars of the cage with his hands. "No! No! No!"

"Yes! Yes! Yes!" Stromboli shouted back at him, pounding his chest. "You now belong to me! We will tour the world! Paris, London, Monte Carlo, Constantinople!"

"No! No!" Pinocchio kept shouting. He had to get back to Geppetto.

"Yes!" Stromboli shouted back, and slammed his fist against the table, making the pile of coins jump. "We start tonight!" He turned, soothed once again by the sight of his gold. Gently he swept the coins into a brown cloth bag. "You will make lots of money . . . for me!"

Stromboli threw the bag of coins to the floor, then picked up a sharp ax and ran his thumb along the blade. "And when you have grown too old . . . I will chop you into firewood!"

Stromboli hurled the ax into an old puppet lying on top of a wooden box. The old puppet quivered almost as if it were alive, and Stromboli laughed fiendishly.

Terrified, Pinocchio started to rattle the bars of his cage. "Let me out of here! I gotta get out! You can't keep me!"

Stromboli spun around and stomped his foot down so hard, everything in the wagon shook. "Quiet! Shut up before I knock you silly."

Startled by the outburst, Pinocchio fell to the floor of the cage. Across the room, Stromboli smiled and blew him a kiss.

"Good night, my little wooden gold mine," he said with a polite bow. Then he turned and, with a menacing laugh, slammed the door behind him.

Atlantia Will Be Mine!

They say that I'm vain~
I would not disagree!
Boy, have I got it~
just look and you'll see!

The Sea King's merdaughters
have only one tail.
But I have eight legs~
and not one horrid scale!

For having me banished
I'll make them all pay!
When I am the Sea Queen
it's *me* they'll obey!

Come, Flotsam and Jetsam,
I'll not turn my back.
My dear little poopsies,
it's time we attack!

They'll never defeat me~
I'll turn them to slime.
Then I'll rule the kingdom
till the end of all time!

MERMAIDS AND MORTALS BEWARE!

WITH A LONG BLACK TENTACLE, URSULA HELD the contract up for King Triton to read. She knew she had him now. Ariel was the Sea King's favorite daughter, and he would do anything—even give up his freedom and power—to save her. What a little fool the girl had been to give up her golden voice and her soul in exchange for legs. And for what! So she could make that human prince fall in love with her. What a pitiful, stupid creature—just like her father.

Sadly, King Triton pointed his trident at the contract. With a bright golden burst, he signed his power away.

"Ha! It's done then!" Ursula chortled triumphantly. She watched with cruel amusement as the magic cocoon that held Ariel now engulfed Triton, transforming him from a mighty king into a shriveled, slimy gray sea creature.

"Daddy?" Ariel gasped in disbelief at what her father had become.

"At last! It's mine!" Ursula cried as she placed the king's gold crown on her own head. She lifted his trident and felt its powerful golden glow light up her face.

"You . . . you monster!" Ariel cried bitterly, and swam at Ursula. She tried to grab the Sea Witch's neck, but Ursula hurled her down onto the sea bottom.

"Don't fool with me, you little brat!" Ursula shouted, brandishing the glowing trident at the mermaid. "Contract or no, I'll blast—" Before the Sea Witch could finish, she felt a searing pain as a harpoon tore across her arm. Glaring up, she saw Prince Eric floating in the water above.

"That stupid fool!" Ursula glowered, grabbing her wounded arm.

"Eric, look out!" Ariel cried, but Ursula quickly muffled her with one of her tentacles.

"After him!" the Sea Witch shouted to Flotsam and Jetsam, her slithering pet eels. Prince Eric swam desperately toward the surface, but he was no match for the long green eels, who quickly caught him.

Ursula smiled as Flotsam and Jetsam pulled Prince Eric down toward the bottom. He was human and therefore would quickly drown.

Suddenly Ariel's friends Flounder and Sebastian swam out from behind a rock and began attacking the eels. As Sebastian pinched Flotsam's tail, Flounder slapped Jetsam's face with his tail until finally, the stunned eels let go of Eric. Ursula gave an unworried smile. Ariel's little friends were merely pests. Aiming the glowing trident at the floating prince, the Sea Witch prepared to destroy him with a powerful burst.

"Say good-bye to your sweetheart," Ursula sneered to Ariel.

But just as Ursula prepared to fire, Ariel lunged and

yanked her white hair, throwing off the Sea Witch's aim. A great ray burst from the trident, but instead of striking Eric, it hit Flotsam and Jetsam.

For a terrible moment the two eels were trapped in the throbbing glow before bursting into a million tiny specks. Ursula dropped the trident and gasped in horror as she tenderly cupped her hands to catch the remains of her favorite creatures.

"Babies!" she moaned grievously. "My poor little poopsies!"

But her grief quickly turned into a vengeful rage. She glared up at Eric and Ariel as they swam toward a small boat floating on the surface. How badly they'd underestimated her powers!

"*Urrrgh,*" Ursula growled, clutching the glowing trident again in her hands. A great cloud of black octopus ink swirled and bubbled as she stirred up the waters around her. Suddenly she started to grow larger and larger as her hate and anger mounted, and finally, with the golden crown still on her head, she rose up through the surface of the water right between the two lovers.

She knew that Eric and Ariel were clinging to the points of her enormous crown. She continued to grow, her body now the size of a dozen sailing ships. She would destroy them once and for all.

"Eric!" screamed Ariel. "You've got to get away."

"I won't leave you!" Eric cried.

He took Ariel's hand, and they leapt off the crown and splashed into the water below. But there was nowhere to hide. Soon Ursula's body filled half the sky. Towering over them, her trident glowed in her huge hand like a solid bar of lightning. With a cruel laugh that sounded like thunder, she stared down at them victoriously.

"You pitiful, insignificant fools!" Ursula's voice boomed out at them as her enormous tentacles emerged from the waters around her. She slapped one tentacle down on the surface, just narrowly missing Eric and Ariel. But no matter, she would get them. Waving her glowing trident through the sky, she created instant thunder and lightning. Driving rains poured down over the sea, and the winds began to howl.

"I am the ruler of all the ocean," Ursula boomed, stirring up giant waves with her tentacles. "The waves obey my every whim!"

A huge wave suddenly curled over Ariel and Eric, tearing them apart and hurling the prince high into the air.

"Eric!" Ariel shouted as he disappeared into the water.

"The sea and all its spoils bow to my power!" Ursula bellowed as she plunged the trident into the water and stirred up an enormous whirlpool. From the ocean bottom sunken ships and treasure were jarred loose from their resting places and were carried upward.

Ariel held on to a rock and tried to hide from the huge Sea Witch and the storm, but it was no use. With a blast from the trident, Ursula shattered the rock, sending Ariel tumbling down through the whirlpool to the ocean floor below.

With a hideous grin on her face, Ursula sent bright blasts from the trident hurtling down at Ariel, but they just narrowly missed her each time. Finally, the Sea Witch decided to finish Ariel once and for all. She raised the great glowing trident over her head, preparing to fling it down at the defenseless mermaid.

"So much for true love!" she shouted with a horrible laugh as Ariel huddled on the sea bottom, waiting for the end.

ME!

I look in the mirror~
what do I see?
No one as handsome,
as gallant as me.

A glistening smile
and big, beautiful eyes,
the women all love me~
I'm such a great prize!

But it's Belle that I want~
my call she must heed!
Why does she ignore me?
All *she* does is *read*!

We'll all storm the castle,
and I'll kill the Beast!
Then I'll marry Belle~
there'll be a great feast!

The townsfolk will marvel
as Belle will be mine.
Two beauties together
until the end of time!

And the only problem
that I can foresee
is who is prettier,
the Beauty, or me?

GASTON WATCHED BELLE'S REACTION to the Beast's image that appeared in the glowing magic mirror. And what he saw made him furious. It actually looked as if she cared for the monster. Suddenly Gaston turned to the crowd of villagers who had gathered around.

"The Beast will make off with your children!" he shouted. "We're not safe until his head is mounted on my wall."

Gaston's plan to frighten the villagers was working. If he couldn't have Belle, then no one would—man or Beast. He began to chant, "Kill the Beast! Kill the Beast!"

One by one the others joined in the chant, and soon every man was armed with a pitchfork or an ax. Gaston knew that Belle would try to stop them, so he locked her and her father, Maurice, in their cellar. "We can't have them running off to warn the creature," he said, turning to the crowd. Then he lit a torch and mounted his horse. Despite the size of the ferocious-looking Beast, Gaston was confident that he could kill him. And then Belle would rue the day she'd rejected his hand in marriage.

The angry mob marched through the dark woods toward the Beast's castle, cutting down a tree for a battering ram

along the way. As they reached the stone bridge that crossed the deep ravine between the forest and the castle, lightning crackled and thunder crashed above. A heavy rain began to splash down out of the black night sky. Gaston dismounted and led the men with the battering ram over the bridge to the great wooden castle doors.

"Take whatever booty you can find," Gaston shouted over the rain. "But remember, the Beast is mine!"

Boooooom! The castle shook as the villagers heaved the heavy log against the doors.

"Kill the Beast! Kill the Beast!" they yelled.

Boooooom! Again the castle doors shook.

On the third attempt the doors flew open with a deafening crash, and the angry mob stormed in. At first everything inside the castle seemed strangely still. Suddenly candlesticks, hat racks, wardrobes, clocks, and dishes began to attack!

The stunned villagers tried to fight back. Gaston had no time to waste with these strange living objects; it was the Beast he sought. Clutching his bow, he slipped away from the battle and began searching the rooms that lined the long stone hallway.

He stopped at a tall green door unlike any of the others. Sensing that this was the Beast's lair, Gaston slipped an arrow into his bow and kicked the door in. The room inside was a dark shambles of broken furniture and tattered tapestries. Gaston spied the hulking figure of the Beast seated near the window.

The villain quietly drew the arrow back and fired.

"*Arrrghh!*" The Beast let out a terrible howl as the arrow struck him in the back and knocked him to the floor.

Seeing that the creature was wounded, Gaston's confidence and determination increased. He bounded across the room and gave the Beast a brutal kick that sent him crashing through the window and onto a rain-slickened balcony. Gaston grabbed a club from the wall and followed.

"Get up!" he shouted. But no sooner did the Beast start to rise than Gaston slammed the club down on his back with a mighty swing.

Wham! The blow sent the Beast sprawling onto a narrow stone buttress high above the ground. The Beast was not such a ferocious opponent after all, thought Gaston.

"Get up!" Gaston cried, and again brought the club down on the Beast's back. The Beast groaned and slumped down on the wet stone. He seemed to have no will to defend himself.

"What's the matter?" Gaston taunted viciously. "Don't tell me you're too kind and gentle to fight back!"

"Nooooo!" a distant voice cried from far below. Gaston was shocked to see Belle riding across the bridge on horseback. She must have escaped from the cellar! He quickly swung the club down on the Beast, hoping to finish him off for good.

But hearing Belle's voice gave the Beast the will to fight back. Suddenly he sprang to his feet, and Gaston gasped at the enormous figure looming over him. He backed away in fear, swinging his club wildly. With a great swipe of his thick arm, the Beast knocked the club away and grabbed Gaston by the neck, lifting him high into the air.

"Let me go!" Gaston cried. "Please don't hurt me. I'll do anything you ask!"

But the Beast grabbed Gaston's throat with his other hand and prepared to snap his neck like a twig.

For a second, Gaston was certain his life was over.

All of a sudden the Beast set him down. "Get out," he said softly.

Bewildered, Gaston staggered away, rubbing his sore neck with his hands. Then he saw the reason the Beast had spared his life. It was Belle, standing behind them, her hair wet and disheveled—with the unmistakable look of love in her eyes. The Beast returned Belle's look.

They would never be together. Gaston would make sure of it! Sliding his hand into his boot, he pulled out a long silver dagger.

"Beast!" Belle cried in warning.

But it was too late. Gaston dove through the air and drove the dagger deep into the Beast's back.

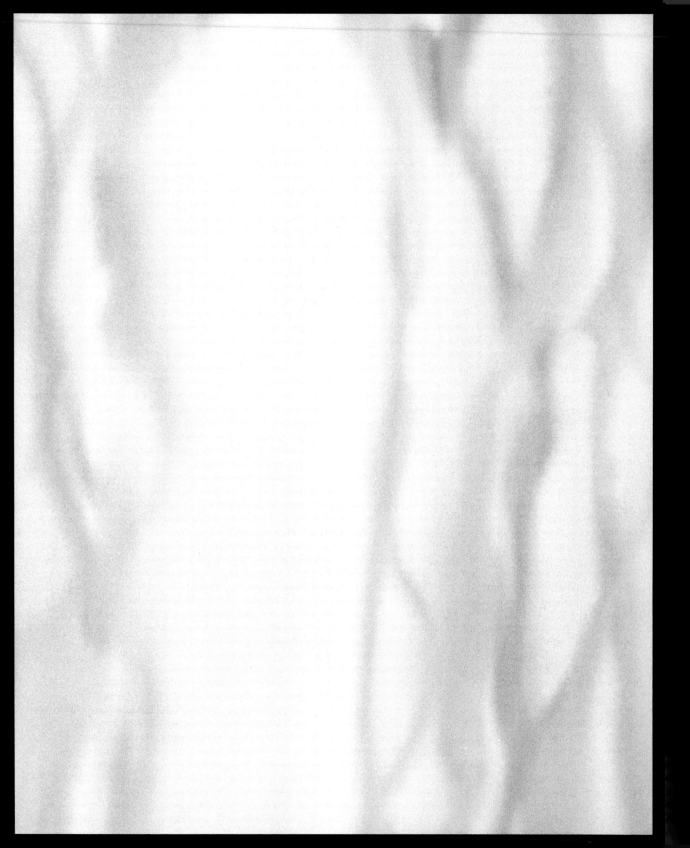